# We Like to Dance

Margaret Clyne

I like to dance.

I do it like this,
*kick, kick, kick!*

I like to dance.

I do it like this,
*tap*, *tap*, *tap*!

I like to dance.

I do it like this, *spring*, *spring*, *spring!*

**spring**

I like to dance.

I do it like this, *spin*, *spin*, *spin*!

We like to dance.

We do it like this, *dip*, *dip*, *dip*!

We **all** like to dance!